INSIDE YOUR AMAZING
SPIDER-MAN
ANNUAL...

▷▷▷

Can you spot the eight Kraven darts hidden inside this Annual?

Write the page numbers in the squares above when you spot a deadly dart!

£7.99

INTRODUCING THE AMAZING WALL-CRAWLING, WEB-SLINGING, WISE-CRACKING SUPER HERO...

THE MAKING OF A SUPER HERO...

THE LIFE OF SHY HIGH SCHOOL STUDENT PETER PARKER, WAS FOREVER CHANGED BY THE BITE OF AN IRRADIATED SPIDER.

ARGH!

THE BITE SOMEHOW GAVE PETER AMAZING SPIDER-LIKE POWERS.

POWERS HE USES TO PROTECT THE INNOCENT.

HOWEVER, THESE ABILITIES HAVE COME AT A COST.

THAT'S THE THIRD DATE YOU'VE HAD TO CANCEL THIS MONTH!

I'M REALLY SORRY, MJ, BUT SOMETHING CAME UP...

AND DR CONNORS TOLD ME YOU FELL ASLEEP IN HIS CLASS AGAIN, PETER...

IF ONLY I COULD TELL HER I WAS UP ALL NIGHT FIGHTING DR OCTOPUS.

REGARDLESS OF THESE PROBLEMS PETER WILL NEVER GIVE UP HIS DUTY TO COMBAT EVIL.

BECAUSE HE KNOWS ALL TOO WELL THE GREAT RESPONSIBILITY THAT COMES WITH THE GREAT POWERS HE HAS BEEN GIVEN!

VITAL STATISTICS

Real Name:
Peter Benjamin Parker

Place of Birth:
Forest Hills, New York, U.S.A.

Height:	5'10"
Weight:	167 lbs
Eyes:	Hazel
Hair:	Brown

NEW YORK

Bronx
New Jersey
Manhattan
Queens
Forest Hills
Brooklyn
Staten Island
Long Beach

ALSO KNOWN AS:
Friendly Neighbourhood Spider-Man, the Amazing Spider-Man, the Sensational Spider-Man, the Spectacular Spider-Man, Spidey, Web-head, Web-slinger, Wall-crawler.

OCCUPATION:
Freelance photographer. Peter is also an accomplished scientist and inventor.

ALLIES:
Avengers, Fantastic Four, X-Men.

EDUCATION:
College graduate (biophysics major), doctorate studies in biochemistry (incomplete).

POWER RANKING:

STRENGTH: 7
SPEED: 5
INTELLIGENCE: 8
DURABILITY: 6
ENERGY PROJECTION: 2
FIGHTING SKILLS: 7

SPIDER-MAN SPIDER-SENSE SPIDER-SENSE SPIDER-MAN SPIDER-SENSE

SPIDER-LIKE ABILITY

Wall-crawling - Can cling to most surfaces.

Super human strength – Can lift up to **10 tons**.

Agility - Known to be **15** times more agile than a regular human being.

Spider-sense – Provides Spidey with an early warning detection system.

GADGETS:
Peter invented various cool devices that are regularly a part of his costume! Here are just a few:

Twin artificial web-shooters worn at the wrists. (A)

Spare web cartridges attached to his belt. (B)

Spider-tracer devices that work in tune with his spider-sense.

Spider-signal light to dazzle his enemies.

Compact camera for those Daily Bugle exclusive shots.

A

B

Looks like good ol' *Spidey* has *Electro* on the ropes! Yep, he sure is gonna have some black 'n' blue bumps on his noggin after--

Whoops! We didn't just drop you into the *tail end of the story*, did we? Eek. Sure *seems* that way, doesn't it?

But *hold on!* Before you throw this mag across the room in a fit of fury and frustration, *turn the page,* True Believers! You'll see we have *far* more respect for you than that!

BITTEN BY AN IRRADIATED SPIDER, WHICH GRANTED HIM INCREDIBLE ABILITIES, **PETER PARKER** LEARNED THE ALL-IMPORTANT LESSON, THAT WITH GREAT POWER THERE MUST ALSO COME GREAT RESPONSIBILITY. AND SO HE BECAME THE AMAZING **SPIDER-MAN** IN

POWER STRUGGLE

SEAN McKEEVER
WRITER

PATRICK SCHERBERGER
PENCILS

NORMAN LEE
INKS

GURU eFX'S HARTMAN and BEVARD
COLORS

TONY S. DANIEL and SOTO'S J. RAUCH
COVER

DAVE SHARPE
LETTERER

TOM VALENTE
PRODUCTION

MACKENZIE CADENHEAD
EDITOR

MARK PANICCIA
CONSULTING EDITOR

JOE QUESADA
CHIEF

DAN BUCKLEY
PUBLISHER

ELECTRO OVERPOWER

Every time I try to make a name for myself, that lucky *punk Spider-Man* gets in my way.

Mocking me. *Humiliating* me in *public!*

That. Is. IT!

It *won't* happen again. This time I'll show them I'm not some *pathetic joke.* I am *not* someone to be trifled with.

I am ELECTRO!

And I deserve some *respect.*

Midtown High

Where's a *super-villain* when you need one?

Aunt May's mortgage payment's coming up, and I haven't had a decent photo op as *Spider-Man* for *days*.

Sure can't sell any pictures if I don't *have* any to sell.

Maybe *Jolly Jonah Jameson* could send me to cover an art gallery, or--

SPLASH!

Hey, Pete-- your *head's* a little wet, pal.

HA!

Yeah. That's real clever, Flash.

Boy, what's it take to get a little *respect* around here? Maybe if I webbed Flash to the flagpole...

CONTINUED ON PAGE 14...

ELECTRO

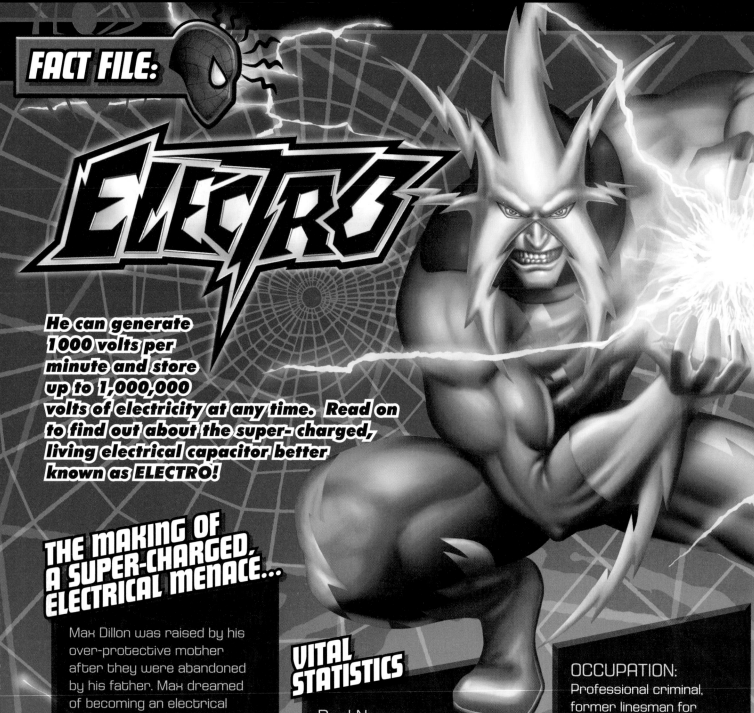

He can generate 1000 volts per minute and store up to 1,000,000 volts of electricity at any time. Read on to find out about the super-charged, living electrical capacitor better known as ELECTRO!

THE MAKING OF A SUPER-CHARGED, ELECTRICAL MENACE...

Max Dillon was raised by his over-protective mother after they were abandoned by his father. Max dreamed of becoming an electrical engineer. However, his mother belittled him, telling him he was not smart enough to pursue such an ambitious career, so he reluctantly took a job as a lineman for an electric company.

During a routine repair to a power line he was struck by a bolt of lightning. The freak accident caused a mutagenic change to his nervous system, allowing him to generate vast amounts of electrical current. Max created a costume and turned to a life of crime as Electro.

VITAL STATISTICS

Real Name:
Maxwell "Max" Dillon

Place of Birth:
Endicott, New York

Height: **5'11"**
Weight: **165 lbs**
Eyes: **Blue**
Hair: **Reddish-Brown**

OCCUPATION:
Professional criminal, former linesman for Consolidated Edison.

ALLIES:
Formerly Exterminators, Sinister Six, Sinister Seven, Sinister Twelve, Frightful Four & Emissaries of Evil

EDUCATION:
High school graduate.

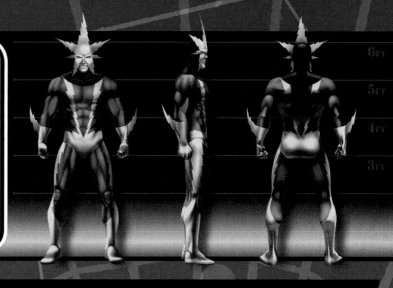

POWER RANKING:

STRENGTH:	4
SPEED:	5
INTELLIGENCE:	5
DURABILITY:	4
ENERGY PROJECTION:	7
FIGHTING SKILLS:	5

A WALKING, TALKING, LIVING CAPACITOR

Micro-fine rhythmic muscle contractions that normally regulate body temperature power his electrical discharges. Storing up to 1,000,000 volts, he can emit lightning arcs from his fingertips at speeds of up to 1,100 feet per second, Wowsers!

MANIPULATING ELECTRICAL DEVICES

Electro can override electrically powered devices such as televisions and cameras and manipulate them with his mind - a handy trait to have as a mischievous villain.

HIGH SPEED TRAVEL

He can travel along conductive materials at speeds of up to 140 mph. Power lines provide the perfect super-charged surfing surface.

WEAKNESSES

When fully charged Electro is in danger of short-circuiting - especially when near water! Zzzzzzttt! Splosh!

...CONTINUED FROM PAGE 11

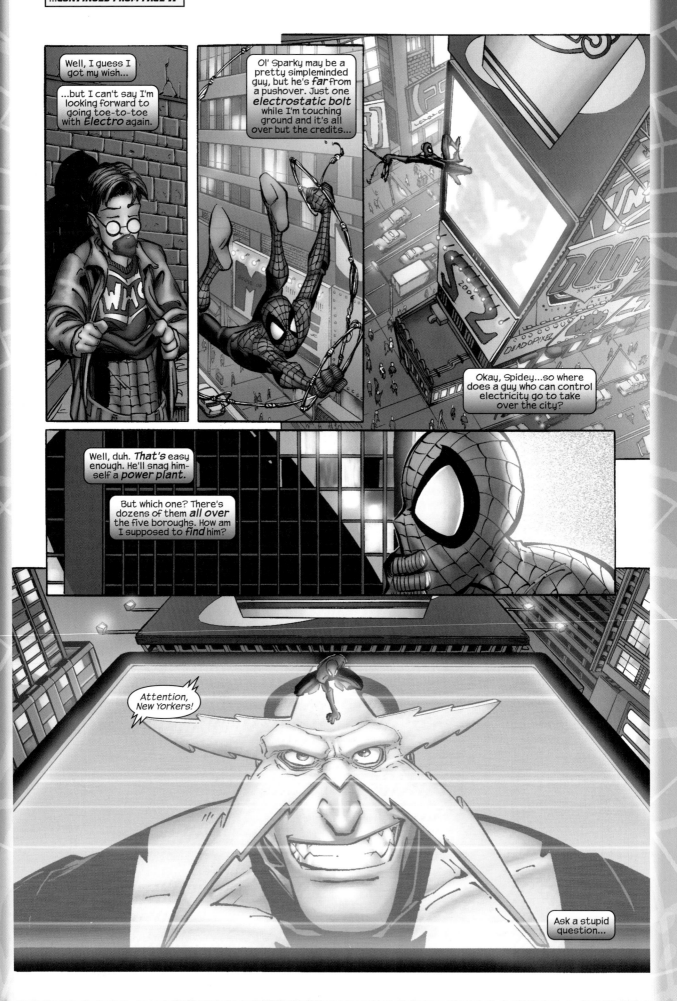

Well, I guess I got my wish...

...but I can't say I'm looking forward to going toe-to-toe with *Electro* again.

Ol' Sparky may be a pretty simpleminded guy, but he's *far* from a pushover. Just one *electrostatic bolt* while I'm touching ground and it's all over but the credits...

Okay, Spidey...so where does a guy who can control electricity go to take over the city?

Well, duh. *That's* easy enough. He'll snag himself a *power plant.*

But which one? There's dozens of them *all over* the five boroughs. How am I supposed to *find* him?

Attention, New Yorkers!

Ask a stupid question...

14

Hey! You heard the dude! Get'cher butt *movin'*, ya bum!

Uh-huh. Love you, too...

THWIP!

Five minutes. He doesn't want me to have time to come up with a *plan*.

Heck, I'll be lucky to *find* him in five minutes. How does he expect me to--

Ooh! Hello, police helicopter.

You know where Electro's at, don'cha? You're gonna take me right to him...

And now you're talking to a helicopter. Great.

Sure enough, we're headed for a power plant. And it looks like ol' Sparky's camped out up on the roof. At least he's finally making it *easy* for--

Hold on...

What's that he's *got* there?

Looks like he's *hardwired* himself right into the plant's *generator*. That would make him a *conduit* for--

Oboy.

FRAKKK!

We're hit! We've lost all power!

Gotta slow that 'copter down!

This is gonna hurt...

CONTINUED ON PAGE 22...

...CONTINUED FROM PAGE 19

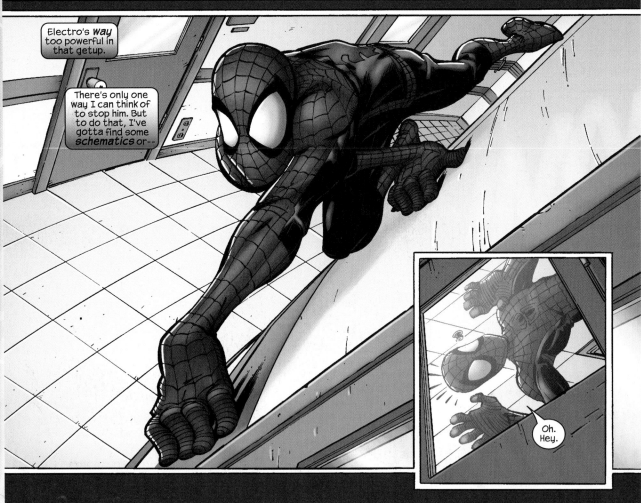

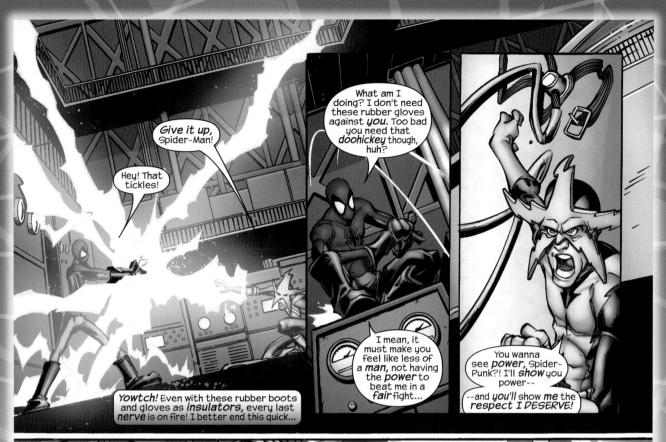

There you go. Drink right outta that faucet, Sparky...

Now, Bill!

Punch it!

ZZAKKK!

Missed me, ugly!

ZZAKKK!

Missed again!

No one can be this lucky! Why won't you fall?!

That was **genius**, Spidey!

By turnin' off the **voltage suppressor**, Electro sucked up so much **power** that he **shorted himself out!**

Aah, yer just bein' **modest**. Yer a **smart** one under that mask!

Yeah, but I couldn't have done it without you and your know-how, Bill.

Hi. 'Scuse me a sec. Do you mind if I just, uh...

And... **cheese!**

CLICK!

Unnnh?

Thanks! I know someone who'll just **love** that pic!

PUZZLES:

Spidey's

Hi gang! OK, so being a hero is not all about how quick, agile and strong you are. You need to exercise your grey matter to keep you mentally alert as well! I've devised some brain-bustin' puzzles based on my run-in with Electro – so let's put your Spidey-sense skills to the test!

1 What does Electro want to take control of?

A) **THE DAILY BUGLE**
B) **THE CITY'S POWER STATIONS**
C) **THE CITY'S POWER SUPPLY**

2 What picture was on the big screen?

a.

b.

c.

3 POWER PLANT PUZZLER

Can you help Spidey get to the power plant in time, avoiding any electric shocks? Follow the power lines to find Electro.

START

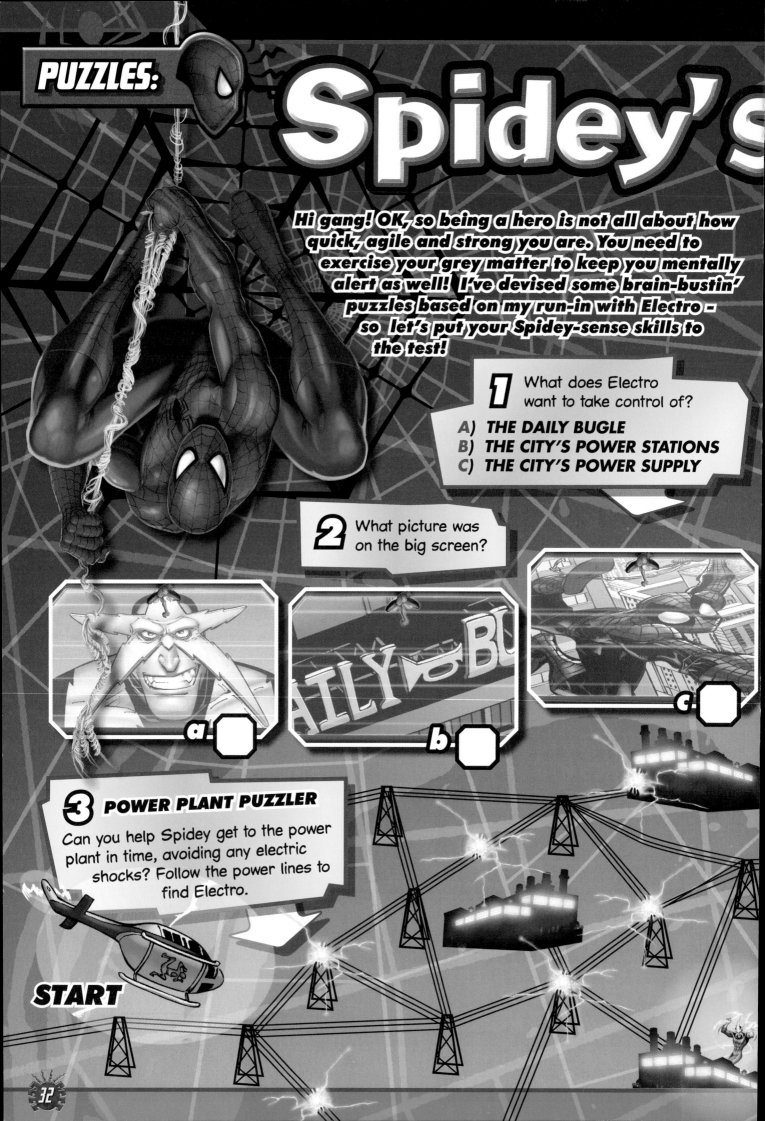

Brain Test!

4 What colour was the cable that connected Electro to the plant's generator?

A) **Blue**
B) **Red**
C) **Yellow**

5 **Fraakk!**

Electro's high voltage shocks have made Spidey see more than one of him! Can you work out which one is an exact match to the original?

Original

a

b

c

6 Can you spot the 5 differences we've made to this picture?

ANSWERS ON PAGE 62

33

Hang on, True Believers--there's some major *turbulence* up ahead for our favorite wall-crawler!

That tough old geezer, the *Vulture*, has publicly announced yet *another* one of his bold plans to commit *grand theft* right out in front of everyone!

This time, his target is a priceless, sacred mask of the Kuba people--on loan from an English museum for an African culture festival in New York City!

And as if stopping Baldy there wasn't enough, Spidey's got *Kraven the Hunter* to contend with, too! How's the web-slinger gonna come out on top this time? *Turn the page* to find out!

BITTEN BY AN IRRADIATED SPIDER, WHICH GRANTED HIM INCREDIBLE ABILITIES, **PETER PARKER** LEARNED THE ALL-IMPORTANT LESSON, THAT WITH GREAT POWER THERE MUST ALSO COME GREAT RESPONSIBILITY. AND SO HE BECAME THE AMAZING SPIDER-MAN IN

VULTURE HUNT!

SEAN McKEEVER
WRITER
PATRICK SCHERBERGER
PENCILS
NORMAN LEE
INKS
GURU eFX'S HARTMAN and BEVARD
COLORS
TONY S. DANIEL and SOTO'S J. RAUCH
COVER

DAVE SHARPE
LETTERER
JAMES TAVERAS
PRODUCTION
NATHAN COSBY
ASST. EDITOR
MACKENZIE CADENHEAD
EDITOR
MARK PANICCIA
CONSULTING EDITOR
JOE QUESADA
CHIEF
DAN BUCKLEY
PUBLISHER

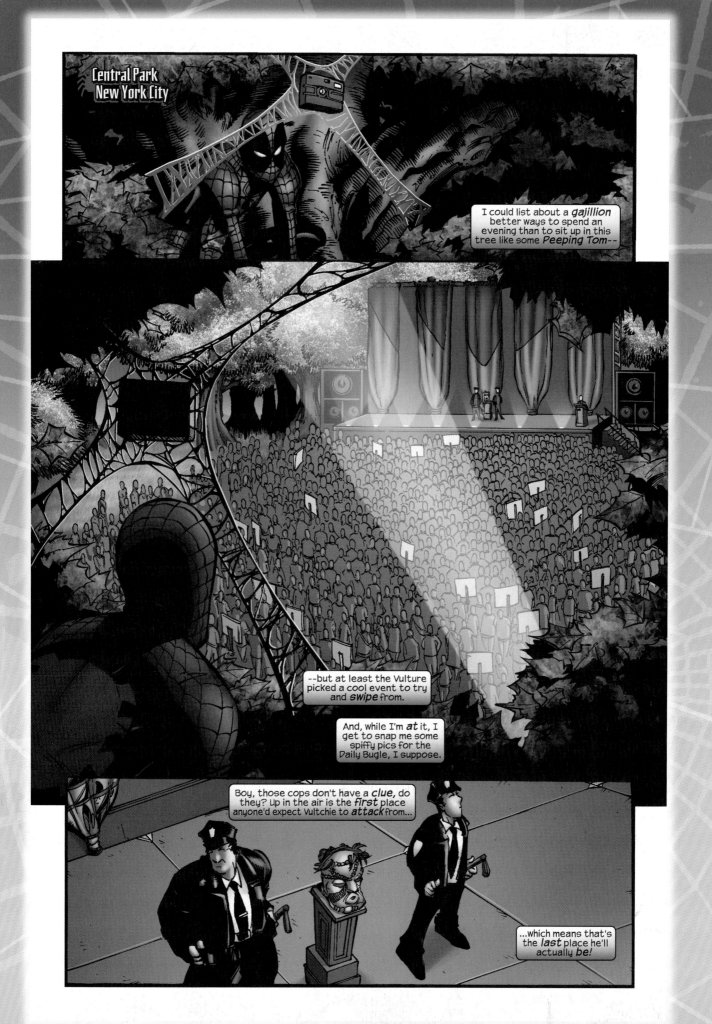

HAHAHAHAHAHA!

All right, who thought this was the *javelin fest*?

The spear belongs to *me*.

It belongs to *Kraven the Hunter*.

Oh, you're kidding me.

So, you're *Vulture's partner* now?

You have a *simple* mind, Spider-Man.

I had come to America to *retrieve* the mask *myself,* but it seems the *old man* has plans for it as well.

Dude, do you not watch the *news?* Vulture only told the *world* what he was up to!

And now I tell you what *Kraven* is "up to":

I am going to *hunt* the Vulture... and then I am going to *take* his prize.

Good-bye, Spider-Man.

Yeah, right. Like I'm letting you--

Hey!

PFF!

PFF!

PFF!

Geez!

What's with the magnesium? Is there a *sale?*

CONTINUED ON PAGE 42...

Big, maniacal and out to prove he's the greatest hunter, Kraven is possibly the most gifted tactician and tracker in the world. Read on to find out more about this hulk of a hunter!

KRAVEN
THE HUNTER

A WORLD CLASS HUNTSMAN...

Unlike other hunters, Kraven is never one to warrant the use of guns or a bow and arrow when his bare hands can do the job just as well - although he has been known to weaken his prey beforehand with poisons!

POWER RANKING:

STRENGTH:	6
SPEED:	6
INTELLIGENCE:	5
DURABILITY:	4
ENERGY PROJECTION:	1
FIGHTING SKILLS:	7

VITAL STATISTICS

Real Name:
Sergei Kravinoff

Place of Birth:
Volgograd (formerly Stalingrad), Russia

POLAND

BELARUS

UKRAINE

MOSCOW

RUSSIA

Volgograd

Height: **6'0"**
Weight: **235 lbs**
Eyes: **Brown**
Hair: **Black**

OCCUPATION:
Professional game hunter, mercenary

EDUCATION:
College educated

ALLIES
The Sinister Six

A POTION TOTING HULK OF A HUNTSMAN

By glugging down mystical potions, Kraven can give himself super human strength, capable of lifting up to 20 tons, and the ability to sprint short distances up to 60 mph. That's almost as fast as a cheetah!

MEDICINE MAN ▶▶▶

Not only can this seeker make mystic potions, he is also familiar with exotic medicines. Just don't get on the wrong side of him, 'cos he is also a dab hand at mixing up dangerous poisons and tranquillisers.

TAMING NATURE

He can battle the most ferocious jungle animals with his bare hands and can also tame the wildest of beasts.

WEAPONS:

Spears
Darts
Axes
Nets
Whips
Poisons
Gases

DID YOU KNOW?

Kraven's lion head vest can release electro-blasts!

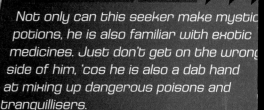

FACT FILE:

A bald-headed, remorseless scavenger. That seems to sum up this feathered forager pretty neatly, but let's find out more about this squawking scoundrel...

THE DESPERADO VULTURE...

Adrian Toomes, a former electronics engineer, is an aging, remorseless killer. He employs a special harness that allows him to fly, plus it also gives him increased strength.

POWER RANKING:

STRENGTH:	3
SPEED:	5
INTELLIGENCE:	4
DURABILITY:	4
ENERGY PROJECTION:	3
FIGHTING SKILLS:	4

VITAL STATISTICS

Real Name:
Adrian Toomes

Place of Birth:
Staten Island, New York City

Height: **5'11"**
Weight: **175 lbs**
Eyes: **Hazel**
Hair: **Bald**

OCCUPATION
Professional criminal

EDUCATION
College educated

ALLIES
The Sinister Six

IN THE FLYING SEAT

Using his harness, the Vulture can fly at speeds of up to 95 miles per hour. He controls his flight with a pair of wings worn on his arms. The harness also increases the Vulture's physical strength. It is estimated that he can lift around 700 lbs, that's about the same weight as a small horse!

VULTURE UNHARNESSED ▶▶▶

Due to prolonged use of the harness, it has recently been revealed that the Vulture can now levitate or float unaided. As with most of his powers, this may fade over time though!

WEAPONS:

Razor-sharp slashing wing tips.

DID YOU KNOW?

The Vulture is an extremely gifted mechanical engineer – handy when trying to construct a flying harness!

...CONTINUED FROM PAGE 39

Uch. *TWO* nutball bad guys. I predict a massive *head-ache* in the near future.

At least I can rush these pics over to the Bugle. A Spidey loss is as good as *gold* to Jonah...

The Daily Bugle

DARK ROOM

Aw, man...!

Is this some kinda *joke*?

These've gotta be the *worst*, most *unprofessional* shots I've ever seen--

--and I've seen 'em *all*!

If you wanna get an *art* degree, Parker, you can do it on your *own* dime! I buy shots that sell papers--*period*!

Speaking of which...

Parker, meet *Andy Anderson.*

Greetings, fellow photog.

Now *these* are front-page shots!

No thanks to my 8.2 megapixel, large-buffer, fast-drive, digital *beauty* here.

The resolution is so high that I can photograph on the *Planck scale!*

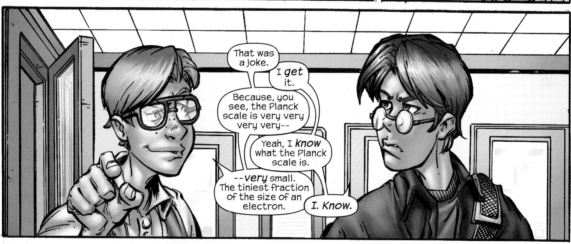

That was a joke. I *get* it.

Because, you see, the Planck scale is very very very very--

Yeah, I *know* what the Planck scale is.

--*very* small. The tiniest fraction of the size of an electron.

I. Know.

*Any*way, thank you for the *commission,* Mr. Jameson.

Fare thee well!

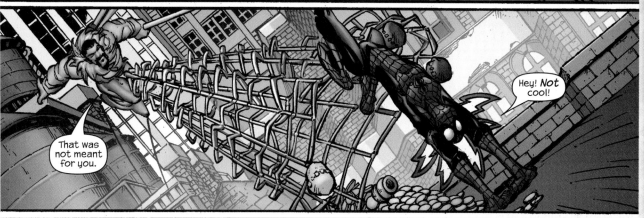

Whoa! This stuff's gotta be worth a *fortune!* What's it doing lying out in the middle of--

Hunh. Well, *that's* odd. It's not valuable at all--just made to *look* that way.

What's going on here?

That was not meant for you.

Hey! *Not* cool!

Why won't you leave me to my *hunt,* Spider-Man?

Uhh...because I find your moustache irresistible? Or *maybe* it's because you're a *wanted criminal.*

Yeah, I'm gonna go with the last one. The criminal thing.

CONTINUED ON PAGE 48...

SPIDEY-SPOTTER

CAN YOU SPOT 10 DIFFERENCES BETWEEN THESE TWO PICTURES?

TURN TO PAGE 52 TO FIND THE SOLUTION, WEB HEADS!

...CONTINUED FROM PAGE 46

Later...

DAILY BUGLE

I don't believe it.

BRING BWOOM BACK
500 YEAR OLD MASK OF KUBA LEGEND IN MUSEUM'S HANDS

The mask really *was* stolen from its people. Kraven was telling the truth.

Kraven...

He's a *bad guy*. I can't team up with a bad guy.

Even if I did, and we got the mask back... *then* what? I can't just *hand* it over to the Kuba. Then *I'd* be guilty of stealing.

And what would I do about *Kraven?* "Hey, thanks for helping me do the right thing. Now let me web you up and *turn you in...*"

What's the right thing to *do* here? I just need some sort of *sign...*

Greetings, Peter Parker.

Great. I'm doomed.

Researching the sacred Kuba *mask*, I see. Nice to see you putting some *effort* into your work.

Excuse me?

I've *already* met with both a Kuba sub-chief *and* the British museum director today and *neither* had any *useful* information, so don't *bother*.

Though I don't know *why* I'm going out of my way to make your job *easier...*

It is a compelling, multifaceted *story*, I suppose, but why would I care about *that?*

I'm an *ace photographer*, not a *journalist*--

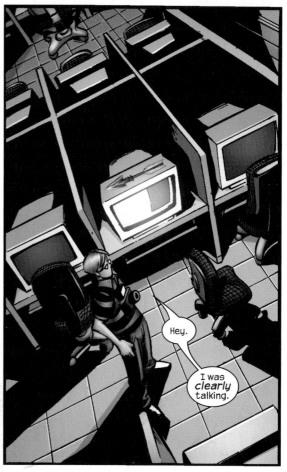

Hey.

I was *clearly* talking.

Later... I'm in.

But two things...

...Vulture goes to the cops... ...and the mask is returned to its *people*. You *don't* get to keep it.

Kraven is a man of his word.

Kraven is a *wanted* criminal.

As are you.

That's completely different. *Jameson* keeps publishing those negative--

Look, I'm not *like* you. End of story.

Mm.

My *hunting prowess* has led me to the Vulture's *nest.* Come. It lies but a short distance from here.

Fine. Let's get this *over* with.

Moments later...

Wow. So...

...when you said "nest," you *weren't* just being pretentiously allegorical.

We proceed as planned. I will get into position.

Yeah, you *do* that...

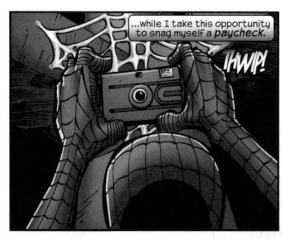

...while I take this opportunity to snag myself a *paycheck*.

THWIP!

Eh? What was that?

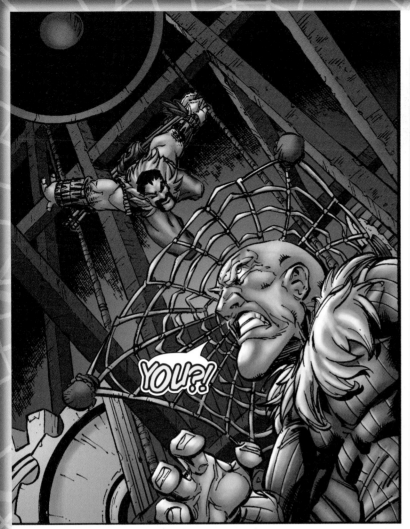

YOU?!

Steal your *own* prizes, Kraven! These are *mine!*

I do not *seek* to possess your baubles, Vulture.

Fine...

...then BUZZ OFF!

What?!

CONTINUED ON PAGE 57...

QUIZ: SUPER HERO

START!

There's been a robbery at the Midtown Bank and you're the first person on the scene. Do you wait for the police to arrive, or start looking for clues yourself?

Look for clues

Wait for the police

You wait for 5 minutes, but there's still no sign of the cops. You could just go home quietly or maybe you'd rather stay around and shout at the cops for being so late?

Wait for the police and tell them

The Police

Go Home

Shout at the police

SPIDER-MAN →▷▷▷

You're a fearless hero who, just like Spidey, is more interested in doing the right thing than chasing fame and fortune.

AUNT MAY →▷▷▷

Like Aunt May, you'd rather have a quiet life, than bother with all this Super Hero sillynesss. Maybe you should try to find a new hobby like knitting.

J JONAH JAMESON →▷▷▷

Oh boy! Remind me not to get on your bad side! You sound like a real old grouch - and just like J Jonah Jameson you've got a bad habit of blaming the wrong people for something they didn't do!

OR SUPER ZERO?!

One of the moneybags the villains stole had a security ink-pack in it that has exploded. If you follow the trail of ink you'll probably be able to find the perp. Do you?

Hey, web heads! Think you've got what it takes to be a hero like Spider-Man? Just take this simple quiz to find out!

Follow the ink trail

You track down the culprit and it's none other than the Shocker. He offers you half the loot if you let him escape. Do you?

Take him down!

Take the money

The Shocker is down and the police have just turned up, along with a reporter from the Daily Bugle. Which one do you talk to first?

The Reporter

KRAVEN →▷▷

You might be brave, but unfortunately you're more interested in your celebrity status than in justice being done, making you most like Kraven the Hunter.

ELECTRO →▷▷

It's easy to see that being a good guy is way down on your list of priorities! Just like Electro, you're only looking out for number one and have no interest in helping others!

PUZZLES:

SPIDEY CENTRAL!

HEY SPIDER FANS, CAN YOU HELP ME SOLVE THESE TRICKY PUZZLES?

BRING BWOOM BACK!

NG BWOOM BACK
YEAR OLD MASK OF KUBA GEND IN MUSEUM'S HANDS

Looks like the Vulture has left behind some decoy masks...

Can you find the actual mask using this newspaper photo example?

A

B

C

SPIDER-HUNT

Spidey needs to follow the Vulture, but he's run into some of Kraven's traps.

Can you find a route that avoids any traps, spears or magnesium flares?

START

FINISH

ANSWERS ON PAGE 62

We had a **bargain!** I held up **my** end, but you--

SPONK!

Oh, whatever.

Kraven-- you're a **criminal.**

I **never** said I'd let you slip away.

Now I'm going to do the right thing and take **this** puppy back to the **festival.**

I'm sure that once I explain everything to the **museum director--**

Naïve child! He would **never** willingly release it to the Kuba!

I'll take my chances, thanks.

Meanwhile, you two can keep each other *company* until the *cops* show up! Bye now!

Muscle-bound moron.

Pathetic old buzzard.

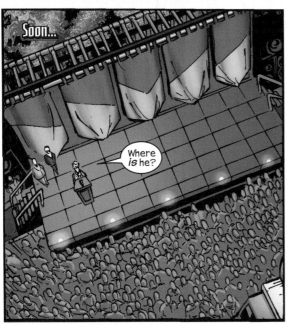

Soon...

Where *is* he?

He *said* he was Spider-Man, and he said he'd be here with the mask. But I don't--

Keep your *toupee* on, Jeeves-- here I am!

As promised, I've come to *return* this sacred mask to a representative of the *museum*...

...so that *they* in turn may return the mask to the *Kuba tribe!* C'monnnn down!

You wait *just* a--

Oh, I can't take *all* the credit. This moment wouldn't have been possible without the insight of *Kraven the Hunter.*

I am most *grateful* for your communiqué, Spider-Man.

Now, you two smile for *all the media from all over the world...!* Hint, hint, pal.

Oh. Uh. Well. Y-yes. O-of course...

The next day...

Decent work, Parker! Better than that *last* batch, at least!

You know, I bet Spider-Man was behind the theft all along so *he* could take the credit!

That doesn't make *sense.* Spidey *shared* the credit with *Kraven*--

"Spider-Man Collaborates with Criminal!"

But--

You *know* how this works, Parker. You get to take the pictures, then I get to write the *headlines.*

Or, I *could* just go with *Andy Anderson's* pictures instead.

Really? You'd run a picture that shows Spidey being *applauded?*

Okay, if that's how you *want* it...

Now just a *minute* there, Parker! I was making a joke!

You *know* I was making a joke!

Parker?

DAILY BUGLE

PARKERRR?

END

Page 32

Spidey's Brain Test!

1 C) THE CITY'S POWER SUPPLY

2 A) ELECTRO

3 START

4 C) YELLOW

5

a   b   c

6

Page 47

SPIDEY-SPOTTER

Page 56 SPIDEY CENTRAL!

START

A

FINISH